THIS BOOK BELONGS TO

_ _ _ _ _ _ _ _ _ _ _ _

For Debs and Caroline,
my cake and coffee besties xx - L.C.

For my wonderful, Mum and Dad x - N.D.

IMPORTANT INFORMATION:
DO NOT EAT! ↘

ORCHARD BOOKS
First published in Great Britain in 2023 by Hodder & Stoughton
2 4 6 8 10 9 7 5 3 1

Text © Lou Carter, 2023 • Illustrations © Nikki Dyson, 2023
The moral rights of the author and illustrator have been asserted.

ISBN 978 1 40835 936 5
Printed and bound in China

MIX
Paper from
responsible sources
FSC® C104740
FSC
www.fsc.org

Orchard Books, an imprint of Hachette Children's Group
Part of Hodder & Stoughton Limited
Carmelite House, 50 Victoria Embankment
London EC4Y 0DZ

An Hachette UK Company
www.hachette.co.uk

www.hachettechildrens.co.uk

OSCAR

the Hungry Unicorn

EATs CAKE

Lou Carter

ORCHARD

Nikki Dyson

It's Princess Oola's birthday today! All her friends have brought presents.

Oola LOVES presents...

MUNCH...

. . . so does Oscar.

The troll gives Oola a homemade card. He cut out the poppy-uppy bits **ALL** by himself. *Such* a clever troll.

(POPPY-UPPY BITS ARE OSCAR'S FAVOURITE.
HE ATE THEM **ALL** BY HIMSELF. SUCH A CLEVER UNICORN!)

Oola will absolutely love these chocolates.
They have been specially magicked up by the witch.

(AND SPECIALLY EATEN UP BY THE UNICORN.)

What about this beautiful bouquet!

WOOF!

The fairies travelled far and wide to fetch the most wondrous blooms from every corner of the kingdom! Everyone loves flowers. (ABSOLUTELY **EVERY**ONE.)

Oi!

MUNCH

MUNCH

Pat is organising the party game!
Oola loves hitting the piñata . . .

SWISH

... Oscar loves **EATING** the piñata.

The king says the party was meant to be for Oola, **NOT** Oscar.

Maybe it's time for Oscar
to have a time out.

LALAA

Ahh that's better.
Now Oola can enjoy the
pirates' jolly birthday music.

But Oola doesn't feel jolly. The party isn't the same without her unicorn.

Maybe the dragon's spectacular light
show will cheer Oola up!

POP!

WOW!

ROCK N' TROLL

BANG!

But no . . . nothing in the
WHOLE WIDE WORLD can
cheer her up without Oscar!

OOOooo!

SIGH

The queen says never mind about Oscar. Chef stayed up all night baking the most **AMAZING** treaty-sweety, hearty-party birthday cake!

WOW

ROCK N' TROLL

But Oola is too sad to eat cake without her unicorn!

(AND JUST WHERE IS OSCAR, ANYWAY?)

OOLA

Luckily, amazing treaty-sweety, hearty-party birthday cakes are Oscar's seventh favourite snack.

Oola says it is the absolute

BESTEST PARTY EVER

now she has Oscar to share it with.

And he is a jolly good
BALLOONICORN too!